NICK JR.

Go Diego Go!

Save the Elephants!

adapted by Alison Inches

based on the teleplay by Ligiah Villalobos

illustrated by Ron Zalme

Ready-to-Read

Simon Spotlight/Nick Jr.
New York   London   Toronto   Sydney

Based on the TV series *Go, Diego, Go!*™ as seen on Nick Jr.®

SIMON SPOTLIGHT

An imprint of Simon & Schuster Children's Publishing Division
1230 Avenue of the Americas, New York, New York 10020

Manufactured in the United States of America
First Edition
2 4 6 8 10 9 7 5 3 1
Library of Congress Cataloging-in-Publication Data
Inches, Alison.
Elephant rescue! / adapted by Alison Inches ; based on the teleplay by
Ligiah Villalobos; illustrated by Ronald Zalme. — 1st ed.
p. cm. — (Ready-to-read)
"Based on the TV series Go, Diego, Go! as seen on Nick Jr."
ISBN-13: 978-1-4169-3821-7
ISBN-10: 1-4169-3821-4
I. Villalobos, Ligiah. II. Zalme, Ronald. III. Go Diego! go (Television
program) IV. Title.
PZ7.I355Sav 2007
2006027045

I am .
DIEGO

This is 👧.
ALICIA

And this is 🐆.
BABY JAGUAR

Today we are in 🌍.
AFRICA

This is our friend .

JUMA

 is an Animal Rescuer

JUMA

too!

 needs our help.

JUMA

The African  are

ELEPHANTS

under a spell.

A mean  turned the

MAGICIAN

 into  !

ELEPHANTS   ROCKS

One  hid from the .

ELEPHANT   MAGICIAN

Her name is .

ERIN THE ELEPHANT

 has a magic .

ERIN THE ELEPHANT   DRUM

The magic  can break
DRUM

the  's spell.
MAGICIAN

We need to take the  to them so they can change back from  to  !

DRUM

ROCKS   ELEPHANTS

We need to go on a safari
to get to the !
ROCKS

will help us.

We are on .

We will go through the .

Then we will cross the .

to get to the giant .

We will save the  !

ELEPHANTS

To the rescue!

On our safari we see animals.

We see  and .
GIRAFFES   ZEBRAS

We see and .
BABOONS   HIPPOS

Here come some  !
LIONS

 says  stomp their feet
JUMA   ELEPHANTS

to scare away  .
LIONS

Stomp your feet like an  !
ELEPHANT

The  ran away!
LIONS

Great stomping like an !
ELEPHANT

is very hot.
BABY JAGUAR

can cool
ERIN THE ELEPHANT   BABY JAGUAR

with her   .
EARS

flap their   to make
ELEPHANTS   EARS

to cool off.
WIND

feels much better.
BABY JAGUAR
Thank you, ERIN THE ELEPHANT !

Come on!

We have to cross the .
LAKE

We need to get the magic
DRUM

to the giant
ROCKS

to save the
ELEPHANTS

The  is big.

LAKE

How will we get across?

 says love to

ERIN THE ELEPHANT   ELEPHANTS

swim.

Swim like an  !

ELEPHANT

We swim all the way
to the giant .
ROCKS
Good swimming!

Oh, no!

The mean !

MAGICIAN

Zap!

The  turned

MAGICIAN   ERIN THE ELEPHANT

into a giant  too.

ROCK

Time to use the magic !

We have to save the !

 as fast as you can!

DRUM

ELEPHANTS

DRUM

It worked!

The magic  broke the
DRUM

spell.

The ELEPHANTS are free!

And the  turned

MAGICIAN

into a 🐜 !

BUG

The  rescue is complete! All of the **ELEPHANTS** trumpet with joy!